children

Translation: Jean Grasso Fitzpatrick

English translation © copyright 1987 by Barron's
Educational Series, Inc.

© Parramón Ediciones, S.A.
First Edition, April, 1985
The title of the Spanish editions is *Los niños*

All inquiries should be addressed to:
Barron's Educational Series, Inc.
250 Wireless Boulevard
Hauppauge, New York 11788

Library of Congress Catalog Card No. 87-11396

International Standard Book No. 0-8120-3850-9

Library of Congress Cataloging-in-Publication Data

Rius, María.
  Children.

  (The Family)
  Translation of: Los niños.
  Summary: Text and pictures show that children, no matter
where, develop more or less in the same way.
  1. Children – Juvenile literature. [1. Growth]
I. Parramón, José María. II. Title. III. Series:
Family (Barron's Educational Series, inc.)
HQ781.R5813   1987   305.2'3   87-11396
ISBN 0-8120-3850-9

Legal Deposit: B-1310-88

Printed in Spain by EMSA
Diputación, 116
Barcelona (España)

8   9   9960   9 8 7 6 5 4 3 2

the family

children

María Rius

J. M. Parramón

BARRON'S

New York • Toronto • Sydney

Right after they're born,
children sleep a lot.

They eat and grow.

They learn to smile.

They learn to recognize people.

And they learn to walk.

When they're two years old, they learn to wash up, comb their hair, and get dressed all by themselves ...

and they're always talking and asking questions.

Whether they're boys or girls...

they all go to school.

They all learn to read and write and count and paint.

They make friends and play together in the playground.

And they all love their families.

They're children—just like you!

CHILDREN

"Children should be brought up in a spirit of understanding, tolerance, friendship between peoples, peace and universal brotherhood, and with the full awareness that they should devote their energies and abilities to the service of humankind."

The Rights of the Child
proclaimed by the United Nations
in the year 1959

Newborn and smiling!

At four to six weeks of age, babies give their first smiles, usually in response to the mother's face. At about two months they begin to utter sounds, and at three months to hear perfectly and turn toward a noise. Later on, they grasp objects, bring them to their mouths, and chew on them. They learn to sit up without help, can crawl by approximately ten months, and at one year old or so can say *Dada* and *Mama* and wave bye-bye. At eighteen months they walk steadily, and at two they talk, gesture, and sing. The development and progress of children during the first years of life are truly extraordinary!

But be careful....They're still children!

As soon as babies learn to walk, to grasp things, and to climb, they are in great danger of accidents. An astonishing number of mishaps take place in the home. Tragedies can occur when a child chokes on a propped-up bottle or pulls a plastic bag over its head. One must try to predict what *could* be dangerous; that means covering electrical sockets, keeping children away from the stove and hot water, and putting gates on staircases and windows.

The drama of the "first day of school"

For some children, the first day of school is not a happy one. It may be the first time the child is separated from the mother, for example, and the first time he or she is faced with a playground full of shouting children. Nursery school can help prepare a child for this experience.

What they like best

To play and enjoy themselves! There are so many ways to have fun: playing games that mother or father or an older sibling enjoys; painting (with lots of paper and colors so they can freely experiment); playing with water in the bathtub or at the seaside; playing with balls; and—of course—watching television.

Is it good for children to watch television?

Leaving children alone in front of the screen can be of great educational value — but only if the programs are selected carefully. There are many excellent educational presentations that teach important lessons and are fun to watch. Many other programs are entertaining and harmless. However, there are some programs that children may find confusing or even disturbing. Whenever possible, children should watch television in the company of their parents, who explain what is going on and answer any questions that may arise.

Childhood can be divided into two stages: early childhood, which includes the years from birth to five, and late childhood, from six to eleven.